The Truth About Ittie Bi

Angela Callard

AUSTIN MACAULEY PUBLISHERS™
LONDON * CAMBRIDGE * NEW YORK * SHARJAH

A CIP catalogue record for this title is available from the British Library.

ISBN 9781398420946 (Paperback)
ISBN 9781398420953 (ePub e-book)

www.austinmacauley.com

First Published (2021)
Austin Macauley Publishers Ltd
25 Canada Square
Canary Wharf
London
E14 5LQ

Angela Callard is a mother of three with a degree in Fine Art from Leeds Metropolitan University. During her 15-year career in children's education, she developed skilled techniques to communicate with children of various ages. She combines these skills with her passion for art and storytelling into the creation of this book, *The Truth About Itty Bitties.*

For Eva, Max and Otis.

I have a tale to tell you and I swear to you it's true.
The grown-ups won't believe it because grown-ups never do.

But children understand that there is magic all around,
If you take the time to notice it can easily be found.

At the end of every garden in the country and the cities,
Live the strangest little creatures who are called the Itty Bitties.

You may not see them straight away or hear their minute voices,
For Itties run and hide from even teeny tiny noises.

Let's place our fingers on our lips and make a shushing sound,
Snuggle down and turn the page, let's see who can be found.

Let's go to a garden where the path is long and winding,
Leading to an orchard where the first Itty is hiding.

A shy and bashful fellow named Twiddly Itty Dee,
His home is nestled in the roots of an ancient apple tree.

He wears a suit made out of leaves, sewn with the finest thread,
Provided by a silk worm who lives near the garden shed.

He rises in the early hours when you are fast asleep,
His job: to wake this silent Earth from a slumber long and deep.

9

The only way this can be done, as you may well have heard,
Is by the gentle music made by every garden bird.

They are his feathered orchestra and he their wise conductor,
As starling, magpie and sparrows sing loud for their instructor.

He'll finish off with merry trills from the cuckoos and the lark,
And knows his job is done as next door's dog begins to bark.

Among the weeds and broken glass of 15 Thistledown Crescent,
Hiding in the shadows lives an Itty most unpleasant.

He sits upon a toadstool throne, long fingers drum his knee,
Dreaming up beautiful mischief, giggling about it with glee.

He wears a tatty top hat, tappety-taps his crooked cane,
Skrumple Itty Snotgrass is this wicked creature's name.

His favourite thing is leaving traps for humans just like you,
With rusty nails and drawing pins and stale old doggy poo.

He leaves them out on paths and steps or right outside your door,
Hoping you will tread on them as your foot steps on the floor.

And as you jump and leap about saying, Ewww! And Errr! And Owww!
He'll clap his hands and dance around, then take a tiny bow.

When his evil deed is done and he's danced his little jig,
He shouts, "It's all the humans' fault for being so dumb and big."

Under a very well-pruned bush that grows gooseberries of green,
In the garden of Your Royal Highness, her Majesty the Queen.

Lives Tallullah Itty Pearldrops, dressed in the finest gown,
Upon her finely coiffured hair sits a splendid acorn crown.

A hoity-toity Itty, high-class and well-to-do,
She can peep out every morning at the most amazing view.

Roses stand like soldiers on guard by gates of gold,
Wearing their dashing red uniforms, smart and handsome and bold.

An army of marigolds stand in lines around a well-kept lawn,
While a marching band of tulips blow their trumpets until dawn.

Each evening after a supper of the finest caviar,
She will walk amongst the flowers softly strumming her guitar.

Every lily, poppy and iris bow down their delicate heads,
As this Itty Bitty royalty strolls past their flowery beds.

Surrounded by rusty old paint pots, long forgotten and thrown away,
Lives an Itty Bitty artist working hard on his craft every day.

For Damian Itty Van Tallent, the circle is his passion,
Magnificent spheres, orbs and hoops for him are all the fashion.

Wearing a smock covered in paint he goes completely dotty,
When he creates a work of art and makes it nice and spotty.

He loves to cut his favourite shape out of the things he sees,
From plants with petals bold and bright and hanging leaves from trees.

It is of course the poor old snails who always get the blame.
"Go fetch the pellets and the salt," the gardeners exclaim.

So next time that you notice circles missing from your flowers,
You'll know an artist was at work there in the early hours.

At night he'll gaze in wonder at the moon up in the sky,
"That really is a masterpiece to look at while I lie."

In a tall apartment block on the south side of the city,
You would not think it possible to find an Itty Bitty.

Well... Once upon a time Miss Rowena Itty Truesong,
Grew tired of the garden she had lived in for so long.

One day by chance a flock of birds had landed in her garden.
She said, "Hello, excuse me, how do you do? I beg your pardon.

I don't suppose you feathered gents would give a girl a ride?
This garden makes me really sad and most unsatisfied."

Away from the gloom of the shadows, up in the sun-lit sky,
She yelled, "It's all so pretty I want to live somewhere this high."

The bird, he knew of just the spot to make Rowena happy,
And flew towards a block of flats (he's such a clever chappie).

A window box! The perfect home, with views for miles around.
How brave she'd been to take the risk and fly there from the ground.

You cannot leave this secret world before I introduce you,
To an Itty like no other, a hero brave and true.

A gargantuan-sized Itty, you would stand there all agog,
He is easily as big as a fair-sized garden frog!

Mr Victor Itty Crabtree, his sheer size sets him apart,
But the biggest thing about him is his kind and gentle heart.

His muscles stand like mountains on his arms as strong as iron,
He would easily win a battle with a dinosaur or a lion.

He uses his strength protecting tiny creatures small and meek,
From vicious crows and ravens who might catch them in their beak.

It is said that once a sly old fox came looking for some dinner,
He thought a juicy rabbit or plump chicken would be a winner.

Our hero swiftly grabbed him by the tail so thick and bushy,
And flung him over the garden wall onto something warm and mushy.

31

So there it is, now you know the truth about Itty Bitties.
Whether in the countryside or smoke-filled dusty cities.

Our friends are here among us, each and every day,
Watching you in your garden as you laugh and run and play.

It's such a wondrous thing to think that right outside your door,
Is a tiny world of magic, that is ready to explore.

So the next time that your Frisbee flies off to the garden bottom,
Or bouncy ball goes missing and lays there all forgotten.

Remember someone's watching as you're searching for your toys,
And listen for the gentle laughs from Itty girls and boys.

And as you rummage through the grass and leaves so brown and crinkly,
Watch out for blinking Itty eyes so small and bright and twinkly.